BARBARA DILLON

MR. CHILL

ILLUSTRATED BY
J. WINSLOW HIGGINBOTTOM

WILLIAM MORROW & COMPANY, INC. * NEW YORK

For Lois
B.D.

To Little Jorge, "Mr. Warmth"
J.W.H.

Text copyright © 1985 by Barbara Dillon
Illustrations copyright © 1985 by J. Winslow Higginbottom
All rights reserved. No part of this book may be reproduced or utilized in any form
or by any means, electronic or mechanical, including photocopying, recording or
by any information storage and retrieval system, without permission in writing
from the Publisher. Inquiries should be addressed to William Morrow and Company, Inc., 105 Madison Avenue, New York, NY 10016. Printed in the United
States of America.   1 2 3 4 5 6 7 8 9 10

Library of Congress Cataloging in Publication Data
Dillon, Barbara. Mr. Chill. Summary: Garrett is astonished when his snow-
man comes to life and announces that his name is Mr. Chill. 1. Children's stories,
American. [1. Snowmen—Fiction] I. Higginbottom, J. Winslow, ill. II. Title.
PZ7.D5791Mr 1985   [Fic]   85-5107
ISBN 0-688-04980-X
ISBN 0-688-04981-8 (lib. bdg.)

CONTENTS

SNOW DAY

When he woke up and peered out his window, Garrett MacBain could not believe how much it had snowed. You didn't even have to turn on the radio to find out whether school would be open. All you had to do was look at the six inches of white stuff that had piled up on the windowsill during the night.

He got out of bed, put on his robe and slippers, and padded down the hall. His father was drinking coffee at the kitchen table. His mother was taking clean dishes out of the dishwasher.

"Looks like you lucked out today, Pal," Mr. Mac-Bain said, wiping his mouth on a paper napkin as he rose from the table.

Garrett went to the window for a closer inspection.

"The trains will be running late," said Mrs. MacBain, carrying a load of cups, hooked over her fingers, to the cupboard. "I wish you could stay home today, Charlie." Snow always worried Mrs. MacBain. She worried about getting stuck in it, slipping on it, and skidding in it. My mother is a born worrier, Garrett thought as he sat down and poured himself some cereal.

"Got to get into town," Mr. MacBain said, patting Garrett's head on his way out of the kitchen. "I've got a meeting at eleven. Has anyone seen my boots?"

"Do you suppose they're still in a packing box?" Mrs. MacBain said. The MacBains had moved to Stonefield from Glen Ridge only two weeks ago, and there were a few boxes no one had gotten around to opening yet.

"I saw your boots in the garage," Garrett told his father, "next to the lawn sprinkler."

"Thanks, son," Mr. MacBain said, returning from the hall in his coat and muffler.

"Walk carefully out there," Mrs. MacBain warned, giving her husband a peck on the cheek. "The sidewalks will be slippery."

"Garr, why don't you give Bruce Biggs a call later?" Mr. MacBain suggested casually, putting on his gloves.

Garrett frowned at the kitchen door as it closed behind his father. Both his parents were at him to get better acquainted with Bruce Biggs. In fact, that had been one of the first things they told him after they picked out the new house in Stonefield. "Guess what?" they said, "there's a boy in fourth grade who lives right next door. Isn't that lucky?" Grownups, thought Garrett, slurping his cereal. Just because a kid happened to be the same age as you, they thought you were going to be his best friend. Back in Glen Ridge, their neighbor across the street had been the same age as Garrett's father. Garrett had never said to his dad: "Why don't you get together with Mr. Bradley? You're both thirty-six. You ought to be friends." Besides, in the three weeks Garrett had been at the Stonefield school, he had noticed a few things about Bruce Biggs. He was the tallest boy in the class. He was a good athlete. He was good at math. And he was popular with everyone, even the girls and Mrs. Fahey, the teacher. You didn't just call up someone like that and say: "Hey, wanna make a snowman?"

Which was why, about a half hour after breakfast, Garrett was out in the frontyard by himself, rolling a ball of snow for the body of a snowman he had already decided would be the biggest one he had ever made. From one side of the yard to the other he rolled a giant snowball, finishing it beneath the big pine tree at the edge of the lawn. Then he rolled a second ball, slightly smaller than the first. Straightening up, he leaned for a moment against the trunk of the pine to catch his breath, blinking as something wet hit him in the eye. It was beginning to snow again. He glanced down at the two balls at his feet. They were so large that lifting the second one onto the first was going to be a problem. As Garrett stood there, wondering how to do it,

Bruce Biggs came out of his garage with a pair of ice skates slung over his shoulders by their long laces. Garrett almost called to him to help with the snowman, but Bruce went right on down the driveway and across the street to the park, never glancing in Garrett's direction. He must have seen me, Garrett thought, because my red jacket really stands out against all this snow. With a sigh, he went into his house to get something to stand on. A minute later he was back out with a kitchen chair. He put the chair under the pine tree and climbed up on its seat. He was now the right height to place the second ball on top of the first but too high to pick it up from the ground. He stepped off the chair, bent down, and with a grunt, gathered the snowball in his arms. Wobbling a little, he climbed back on the chair and managed somehow to heave the snowball into place on top of the first. Then he hopped down again and quickly rolled a third snowball for a head. By standing on tiptoe on the chair seat, he was able to put the head on the body. Then there it was, an enormous snowman. Now for the fun part—finding twigs for arms and something for eyes. He turned as he heard footsteps behind him. It was his mother, bundled up in her coat.

"Oh, Garrett!" she exclaimed, looking at his snowman. "How in the world did you ever build anything that size?"

"I'm not sure," Garrett admitted, stepping down from the chair.

"He should have special eyes," Mrs. MacBain decided, squinting at the snowman, "and I think I have just the thing, those big jet buttons I bought last fall and never used." She hurried back into the house to get them.

While she was gone, Garrett went in search of twig-arms. Somehow it didn't surprise him at all when he found two that were exactly right on a poplar tree at the side of the house. It was almost as if this snowman was helping to build himself.

A moment later his mother came back carrying the buttons and a pink scarf clutched in one of her mittens. The buttons were big and shiny, and when Garrett, again standing on the chair, placed them on the snowman's face, they looked almost like real eyes. He stuck in the twig-arms, and his mother wound the scarf around the snowman's neck.

"He needs a mouth," said Mrs. MacBain, and she quickly sculpted with her hands a kind of jack-o'-lantern mouth with a few little square teeth in it.

"That looks great," Garrett said. "Is there any film in the camera? I want to take a picture of him before he melts."

"I'm sure there are a couple of shots left, but in this weather you don't have to worry about melting, believe me." Mrs. MacBain looked at Garrett's mittens and frowned. "Your gloves are practically frozen to your hands, Garr," she said, remembering to worry again. "Come inside this minute and take them off. I'm going to heat up some soup for lunch."

"See you later," Garrett called to the snowman,

looking at him over his shoulder as he picked up the kitchen chair and followed his mother to the house. If he hadn't known better, he would have sworn the snowman winked at him with one of his shiny button-eyes.

MR. CHILL MAKES THE SCENE

In the afternoon the sun came out, and except for a few remaining clouds, the sky turned bright blue. Garrett went out to the yard with his camera and took pictures of the snowman from different angles. Later, as it began to get dark, he switched on the outside lights on either side of the front door. In the shadow of the pine tree, his snowman looked even bigger than it had by day. Garrett could hardly wait for his father to see him.

"Dad, did you see my snowman?" was the first thing Garrett asked as soon as Mr. MacBain arrived home at six-thirty, stamping the snow from his boots.

"Did I ever!" Mr. MacBain said. "How did a guy your size ever build a guy that size?"

"I stood on a chair to put the body together," Garrett said.

Mr. MacBain gazed thoughtfully out the kitchen window. "You know, I had the strangest sensation coming up the driveway just now."

"I hope you weren't walking too fast," Mrs. MacBain said quickly. "You have to be extra careful in cold weather like this."

"No, what I meant was, I thought Garrett's snowman waved at me. For a second I thought I saw one of those stick arms raised in a greeting."

"Really?" said Garrett, thrilled that the snowman seemed as real to his father as he did to him.

"Well, as long as you didn't slip and fall," said Mrs. MacBain, carrying her husband's coat to the hall closet. "We're having meat loaf for supper."

Garrett took a final peek into the yard before he hopped into bed at eight-thirty. His room was on the first floor, and as he opened his window a crack he could see the front lawn quite clearly. The night sky was full of stars, and a flat white moon shone coldly. Garrett climbed into bed, thinking about his old room in Glen Ridge. He wondered if Bruce Biggs was in bed, too, and if he'd had a good time today skating with his friends. Then there was a sharp scratching sound at the window. Garrett was startled. A branch of a tree? he wondered. But there were no trees that close to the house. There it was again. He got out of bed and went to the window.

On the other side of the glass a big, white moon face

with shiny black eyes was staring at him. Garrett clapped his hand to his mouth, muffling the cry of surprise that rose in his throat. Two stick arms reached out, stick fingers tried to raise the window higher. "Help me get this thing up, please," said an eager voice. Garrett pushed the window up a few more inches. The snowman peered into his room with interest.

"I've been wondering what the inside of your house looked liked, after staring at the outside all day," he said. "Do you know what my name is?"

Garrett shook his head.

"Mr. Chill," the snowman told him proudly.

"I'm Garrett," Garrett whispered, wondering if he could be dreaming.

"I know," said the snowman. "I heard your mother call you that this morning. Oh, and speaking of your mother, I don't like her taste in scarfs. This pink thing has got to go."

Garrett watched in astonishment as Mr. Chill plucked off his muffler and handed it to Garrett through the window. "Your dad's scarf was neat, I thought. Red, that's my color. Could you please bring it out with you?"

"Bring it out with me when?" Garrett asked.

"Now."

"I can't come out now."

"Of course you can," Mr. Chill said. "I've been wanting to play all day. Get your coat and come on."

What am I waiting for? Garrett thought to himself.

When will I ever get another chance to play with a real snowman? "I'll see you in a minute," he told Mr. Chill.

From his closet floor he pulled out his favorite shirt, which he put on over his pajamas along with a pair of jeans. He crept down the hall, careful to avoid the floor board that creaked when you stepped on it. Two coat hangers jangled together as he took his ski jacket from the hall closet. He held his breath for a second or two, half expecting to hear his mother call: "Garr, is that you?" Then he grabbed his hat and mittens and let himself quietly out the front door.

The moon-drenched lawn was deserted. The snowman was nowhere in sight. Garrett looked down at the ground. He could see strange tracks in the snow, wheeling in a zigzag from the pine tree to his bedroom window and then around the corner of the house. Baffled, he followed the tracks to the garage where he found Mr. Chill examining the rear end of their station wagon.

"Look at this green thing I found," he told Garrett. "It's bigger than I am. What is it?"

"It's an automobile," Garrett told him, staring into Mr. Chill's black eyes.

"How about this?" the snowman asked, moving to a wall shelf.

"That's a watering can. Mr. Chill, can I ask you something?"

"Sure," said the snowman, knocking a clay flower-pot to the floor.

"How come you can talk and move around?"

"Where's your dad's scarf?" Mr. Chill asked, picking up a trowel. "I thought you were bringing it out."

"My dad really likes his scarf," Garrett said. "I can't give it to you. How come you can walk and—"

"You'll have to get me one somewhere else then," Mr. Chill said.

"I haven't got any money," Garrett told him patiently. "How come you walk and talk?"

"How come you can?" Mr. Chill shrugged his big, white shoulders. "I was born inside a great storm cloud," he declared. "Down through the winter sky I tumbled onto your front lawn, nothing more than a heap of ice crystals till you put me all together. You did a pretty good job, too, except for the feet."

"I never thought about feet," Garrett confessed.

"Try walking without them," Mr. Chill told him. "You have to roll along or bowl along. It's not easy."

"Can I ask you another question?"

"Okay," the snowman said, making a lunge at a rake hanging on the wall.

"Well, I was wondering how I could build such a big snowman," Garrett said. "I don't think even my dad could have made one any bigger."

"Probably not," Mr. Chill agreed. "I helped you, Garrett. I was thinking: 'Great, Huge, Gigantic, Stupendous Mr. Chill, that's me.' "

Garrett took off his mitten and touched Mr. Chill. It was hard to believe that the snowman he had made this morning with his own two hands was standing inside the garage, chatting with him.

Suddenly Mr. Chill discovered a small hand saw of Mr. MacBain's. "Just the thing," he said, lifting it from the shelf. "Garrett, could you make a nice little notch with this and then mold two legs? They don't have to be fancy, but I want them to be strong." He thrust the saw into Garrett's hands.

"It won't hurt you?" Garrett asked.

"Of course not," Mr. Chill assured him. "Let's go."

Garrett switched on the garage light and gingerly sawed a groove about a foot long at the base of the snowman. Then he hollowed out with his hand two stumped legs with a few toes at the end of each.

"Wow, that looks really cool," he said, stepping back to admire his work.

"Cool?" Mr. Chill said quickly. "That means good?"

Garrett nodded his head.

"Cool," Mr. Chill repeated. "I like that. I'm cool, real cool. Come on, let's play." And he happily moved forward on his new feet.

By the light of the moon, Garrett showed Mr. Chill around. The snowman asked question after question about trees, the bird feeder, the birdbath, the bare garden at the side of the house. He loved the swing set and the sandbox, now piled with fresh snow.

"The people who lived here before had two little kids," Garrett explained, sitting down next to Mr. Chill on the wooden seat of the sandbox. But the snowman was too busy scooping out snowballs to answer. Garrett, to be polite, helped make some, too.

When at last they had gotten a big pile of them, Mr.

Chill sat back and said: "We've got to put these some place safe."

"Why?" asked Garrett. "There's tons of snow around. We can make lots more anytime we want."

"I want to keep these," Mr. Chill insisted. "Take them into your house."

"They'll melt in the house," Garrett explained gently.

"All right, let's swing then," Mr. Chill said, suddenly losing interest in the snowball project. "Show me how."

Garrett felt a yawn coming. "Just for a minute," he told the snowman. He was beginning to feel a little sleepy. Mr. Chill stumped to one of the two swings and sat down on the seat. Garrett gave him a few pushes, told him about pumping, and got on the other swing. Together they glided back and forth, in and out of the moon shadows. Garrett put his head back and gazed up at the sky and the frosty stars above him. Whoever would have thought that he, Garrett Evans MacBain, would be swinging through the winter night with a snowman?

"Watch this," Mr. Chill said, and all at once he heaved himself off his swing and went flying through the air, landing with a thud several yards away.

"Are you okay?" Garrett asked, dragging his feet along the ground to stop the swing.

"I think so," Mr. Chill said, "except one of these things fell off."

"That's your right arm," Garret told him, picking up

the twig from the ground. With a grunt, he slipped his own arms under the snowman and hauled him to his feet. "You've got to be more careful," he warned, sticking the arm back into Mr. Chill's side.

"You don't ever have to worry about me," Mr. Chill told him cheerfully. "I'm indestructible. As long as there is just one little piece of me left, I'll be fine. I'll probably be around forever. What shall we do now?"

Garrett thought it was kinder not to tell Mr. Chill about warm weather and thaws. He felt another yawn coming on. "I'm going back to bed," he said. "It's freezing out here, and besides, I have to get up and go to school tomorrow."

"What's school?" asked Mr. Chill.

"A place where kids go to learn stuff," Garrett explained. "So long, see you tomorrow."

"I'm lucky, I already know everything," Mr. Chill said.

"That's what he thinks," Garrett muttered, making his way across the lawn. He opened the front door and was about to step inside when the snowman called to him. "Garrett, don't leave me out here, I'm afraid."

Garrett stopped in his tracks and turned in surprise to look at his friend. "Afraid of what?" he asked, lowering his voice cautiously.

"The thing in the tree," Mr. Chill mumbled.

"What thing in which tree?"

"That great big dark thing over there." Mr. Chill raised one arm and pointed toward the Biggses' lawn.

"I don't see anything," Garrett said, and then suddenly laughed as he realized what Mr. Chill was pointing to.

"That's just Bruce Biggs' tree house," he explained.

"How come it wasn't there before?" Mr. Chill asked suspiciously.

"It was, but probably you had so many new things to look at you missed it in the dark," Garrett told him.

"Why does Bruce Biggs live in a tree?" Mr. Chill persisted.

"He doesn't, the tree house is just a place to play. I'm going in now. Good night."

"Good night, Garrett. Garrett?" Mr. Chill said quickly.

Garrett paused with his hand on the doorknob. "What?" he asked patiently.

"Leave a little light on in your room that I can see, okay?"

"Okay," Garrett agreed. "Good night, Mr. Chill." The last thing he saw was Mr. Chill waving to him.

THE TREE HOUSE

"What happened to your snowman's scarf?" Mrs. MacBain asked the next morning at breakfast. She and Mr. MacBain and Garrett peered through the kitchen window at Mr. Chill, who was back under the pine tree looking as though he had been there all night.

"I thought I'd wear that scarf to school today," Garrett told them.

"You in a pink scarf?" said his father, looking surprised.

"With a red jacket?" asked his mother.

"My neck gets cold sometimes," Garrett said, turning from the window. "Oh, I don't think I told you, the snowman's name is Mr. Chill."

"I love it," said his mother. "Who thought that up?"

"He did, I mean I did," Garrett corrected himself quickly. "Now where did I put my math book?"

All during school Garrett thought about Mr. Chill. In the light of day it hardly seemed possible that he had been playing with a snowman the night before. He found himself longing to tell somebody. In fact, he almost spilled the beans to Bruce Biggs when the class went to the art room after lunch. Garrett, hard at work on a picture of a spaceship whirling through a starry sky, suddenly realized Bruce was standing in back of him.

"Hey, that's really cool," Bruce said, leaning closer to examine the helmeted head Garrett had sketched into his spaceship's cabin. "I wish I could draw stuff like that."

"It's not so hard," Garrett said modestly, though he did feel that his picture was turning out pretty well.

Bruce hesitated for a moment and then asked: "Were you out in your yard last night at about nine-thirty?"

Garrett considered for a moment. "I don't know where I was at nine-thirty," he said, which was true because he didn't have a clock in his room or a wristwatch either.

"I thought I saw someone out on your lawn," Bruce mumbled, giving him a slightly strange look. Garrett just shrugged and went back to adding more stars to his drawing.

Later, Garrett was glad he hadn't told Bruce or anyone else about Mr. Chill, because when he got home from school and tried to talk to the snowman, all he got was silence. Had he been dreaming last night after all? He couldn't have been. He could still pick out Mr. Chill's strange footprints on the front lawn.

For once, Garrett was eager for bedtime to roll around. Before eight-thirty he had switched off his light and gotten under the covers. Should he wait to see if Mr. Chill would come to his window? No, he decided, and hopped out of bed just in time to see the snowman walking toward the house. Garrett cupped his hands to his mouth and called through the window. "I'll be right there." He threw on his clothes and tiptoed down the hall. Just as he was reaching into the closet, he heard the den door open. He dived in among the coats and boots, holding his breath as his father passed within inches of him on his way to the kitchen. Garrett heard the refrigerator door open. His father was fixing himself a snack. He stepped out of the closet and slipped through the front door. Mr. Chill was waiting for him on the front steps.

"Can you still talk?" Garrett asked him. "I was worried when you wouldn't say anything to me this afternoon."

"I was busy thinking," Mr. Chill replied, "and then just as I was about to ask, 'Did you learn anything in school today?' that other boy cut across the lawn. The one with the big house in the tree."

"That's Bruce Biggs. He's about the most popular boy in my class."

"Popular?"

"Popular means he has a lot of friends," Garrett said.

"How many friends do you have besides me?" Mr. Chill asked.

"Well, see, I just moved to town three weeks ago," Garrett told him. "Back in Glen Ridge I had lots and lots of them."

Mr. Chill considered this for a moment. Then he said, "Let's go up to the house in the tree." Garrett looked across the dark lawn to the Biggses' property. "I think Bruce saw me last night," he said. "If he sees me again, he'll begin to wonder."

"We'll just stay for a minute." The snowman began shuffling determinedly toward the Biggses' property.

At the foot of the big maple he paused, waiting for Garrett. "How do we get up there?" he asked, looking suspiciously at the ladder nailed to the trunk.

"Like this," Garrett said, setting first one foot and then the other on the snowy rungs. Behind him, he could hear the soft thud of Mr. Chill's feet.

"Guess what," the snowman said as he arrived breathlessly at the top. "Ladders make my head feel funny."

"You're just a little dizzy," Garrett said, taking a guilty look around. If Bruce found out two strangers were up here snooping, he wouldn't be too pleased.

"See me sitting, Garrett," said Mr. Chill, planting himself on the small wooden table in the middle of the tree house.

"Chairs are for sitting," Garrett told him, pointing to one beside the table.

Mr. Chill hopped off and plunked down in the chair. "What's that thing on the wall?"

"It's a poster of a racing car," Garrett told him.

Suddenly Mr. Chill reached out and plucked an icicle from the roof of the tree house. "Something to eat," he said. "Want one?" He snapped off another for Garrett. "Now I will tell you my plan for getting a new muffler," he said, crunching the icicle between his jack-o'-lantern teeth. "Tomorrow we will give out snowballs to people who wear nice scarves. They will give us the nice scarves for the snowballs," he explained as Garrett gave him a puzzled look. Garrett was about to say no one would give away a muffler for a snowball, when an idea popped into his head. He looked at Mr. Chill fondly. "I think maybe I could make that scheme work," he said. "I could put some sugar and food coloring in the snowballs. They'd sell much better that way."

Garrett stopped talking at the sound of footsteps crunching across the lawn. The beam of a flashlight moved through the bare branches of the tree, catching Garrett leaning against the table and Mr. Chill sitting on the chair.

"Holy moly!" Bruce Biggs exclaimed. "How'd you ever get that snowman up there, MacBain?"

"I climbed up," Mr. Chill called down to him, "but I hate ladders."

"I can explain everything," Garrett gulped, not at

all sure that he could, and quickly began backing down the ladder.

"You come too, Mr. Chill," he called when he reached the ground. Mr. Chill got up from his chair and peered uncertainly after Garrett. All at once he toppled forward and came crashing through the branches, hitting the ground with a muffled thud. To Garrett's horror, the snowman's head bounced off and rolled along the lawn right to Bruce Biggs' feet.

"Oh, Mr. Chill!" Garrett cried. He didn't know if he should right the body first or pick up the head. "Help me," Garrett called, but Bruce Biggs just stood open-mouthed, staring at the broken snowman.

"He can talk?" Bruce asked finally. He looked as if he might turn and bolt into the house.

"Not if his head's come off, he can't," Garrett said impatiently. "Can you please help me put him back together?"

Bruce laid down his flashlight and moved warily toward Garrett, who was struggling to raise the snowman into a standing position. Together they stood Mr. Chill up.

"How are we gonna get the head back on such a tall body?" Bruce asked.

"I used a chair the first time," Garrett told him.

"I think there's a stepladder in our garage," Bruce said, and went off to get it. He propped the ladder close to Mr. Chill's body; Garrett gathered the snowman's head in his arms and handed it up to Bruce who shoved it into place.

"What happened?" Mr. Chill asked as Bruce climbed down. "One minute I was flying like a bird, the next minute everything went black."

"That's because your head fell off," Garrett told him crossly. "Mr. Chill, you've got to stop leaping off into space."

"I know," the snowman said humbly. He turned to Bruce: "Nice place you've got up there."

"I don't believe I'm hearing a snowman talk," Bruce said. He looked accusingly at Garrett. "You're not a ventriloquist or something, are you?"

Garrett shook his head. "Last night he came to my window and asked me to come out and play."

"You can play with us, too," Mr. Chill told Bruce. "It would be nice for Garrett, because he doesn't have any friends here except me."

"Mr. Chill!" Garrett looked down at his boots in embarrassment, but the snowman was already pointing to something in Bruce's backyard.

"What is that thing?" he asked Bruce.

"That's my little sister's seesaw," he murmured, still looking stunned.

"How does it work?"

"Come on, let's show him," Garrett said. As Mr. Chill tramped on ahead, Garrett whispered to Bruce, "I don't want anyone else to find out about this. It wouldn't be special anymore if a whole lot of people found out."

"But what about our parents?"

"We shouldn't even tell them." Garrett said.

"Come on," Mr. Chill called impatiently. "I want to see this seesaw."

A minute later they had all climbed on the seesaw together. The boys' combined weight on one end almost perfectly balanced Mr. Chill's on the other; as the three riders bobbed up and down, Garrett told Bruce his plan to earn money for a scarf for Mr. Chill.

"I guess if we used the snow on that second-story porch outside my parents' bedroom, it would be clean enough to make snow cones," Bruce said. "But you can bet our parents would go into orbit if they knew we were selling it."

"The snow that I fell to earth in is cleaner than clean," Mr. Chill declared. "It was a special, once-in-a-lifetime snow. Anything that falls later on I can't make any promises about. But what's on Bruce's porch, my snow, is as pure as I am, and that's pretty pure. So on with the sale!"

✳ THE ✳
SNOW CONE SALE

"Why didn't you get me up, Mom?" Garrett demanded the next morning. He rushed downstairs in his pajamas. "I have stuff to do."

"It's Saturday, so I let you sleep," Mrs. MacBain said. She looked up from the pile of wash she was sorting at the kitchen table. "What kind of stuff?"

"Bruce Biggs and I are having a sort of sale," Garrett said. He poured himself a glass of apple juice.

"Really?" Mrs. MacBain looked at Garrett. "When did you two decide all this?"

"Last night," Garrett said, sitting down at the table. "I mean, er, yesterday afternoon, late, after school," he corrected himself.

"I had no idea you and Bruce even talked to each

CONES

Italian Ice
CONES
1 SCOOP — 10¢
DOUBLE SCOOP 15¢
40

PAINTING BY NUMBERS

other," his mother said, sounding pleased. "What are you selling?"

"Different things," Garrett mumbled and ran upstairs to get dressed.

Two hours later, at the bottom of the MacBains' lawn, a cardboard lemonade stand had been set up. Garrett's father hadn't wanted to take the stand when they moved; how glad Garrett was now that he had insisted they keep it. He made a sign with a magic marker: ITALIAN-ICE CONES. ONE SCOOP, 10¢. DOUBLE SCOOP, 15¢ and tacked it up over the one that read: LEMONADE, 5¢ A GLASS.

"Of course our snow isn't really Italian," Garrett said, "but I bet it's just as good as what they sell in the supermarket."

"That stuff probably isn't really Italian, either," Bruce pointed out, which made them both feel better about the sign. Luckily Bruce's mother had a whole box of ice-cream cones left over from a Cub Scout picnic. They stacked the cones on the counter, next to big mixing bowls filled with snow that Garrett had sweetened with a little sugar and tinted with red, green, and blue food coloring. He had even added some mint extract to the green snow. A bowl of purple snow Bruce made by mixing red and blue food coloring had come out looking murky, so he and Garrett were holding it aside, just in case they ran out of the other colors.

So that he wouldn't feel he had lied *completely* to his mother Garrett brought out a few items to sell: a bag of unopened candy corn from Halloween, an airplan model he'd never taken out of its box, blue glitter shoelaces, and a paint-by-numbers set he'd won at a school fair back in Glen Ridge. Bruce contributed a pack of baseball cards, a hamster run, and a Michael Jackson poster.

Only minutes after the stand was set up and the ice made, the first customers arrived, two boys carrying skates. Using his mother's ice-cream scoop, Garrett served up double dips. Three girls in his class appeared next, pulling sleds. When they saw Bruce, they giggled and shoved each other and dropped their money in the snow. They had only fifteen cents between them, so Garrett gave them a triple dip of Bruce's purple ice, which they all shared.

Soon the boys had so many customers, it was all they could do to make the cones and count out the right change. The hamster run was sold almost immediately, followed by the glitter laces and the paint-by-numbers set. Two girls almost had a fight over the Michael Jackson poster. Mrs. Moon, a neighbor who walked her Scottie twice every day, paused to admire their stand. Although she had gray hair and looked very old to Garrett, she was dressed like he and Bruce were, in jeans and hiking boots and a ski jacket.

"Well, this is certainly an unusual idea," she said, holding a green snow cone for her dog, Hotshot, who lapped at it eagerly. She glanced up at Mr. Chill standing under the pine tree, his black jet eyes sparkling in the cold sunlight.

"That's a wonderful snowman, Garrett. I hope you've taken a few pictures of him."

"Yup, I have," Garrett told her, pleased at the compliment. "Mom took the film to be developed this morning."

"I'd like to see those snowman prints when they're developed."

"I'll bring them over," Garrett promised as Mrs. Moon gave a tug on Hotshot's leash and led him toward home.

From the living-room window, Garrett's parents were watching all the activity on the lawn, or what they could see of it, through the trees. Suddenly Mr. MacBain leaned closer to the window. "Didn't Garrett build his snowman facing toward the house, Margo?"

"Yes, of course, he did. My gosh, he's turned Mr. Chill around somehow." Mrs. MacBain shook her head with a laugh. "Isn't that just like Garrett? He probably wanted his snowman to be able to watch the sale."

Mr. MacBain slipped on his glasses. "Is that an ice-cream scoop he has in his hand? It looks like he's handing a cone to a girl in a blue parka," he observed in a puzzled voice. "Come on, Margo, let's check this out for ourselves."

"Garrett, what is all this?" he asked his son a moment later as he and Mrs. MacBain stood reading the sign over the lemonade stand.

"Italian Ice?" Mrs. MacBain said in surprise.

"It's really clean snow we collected from my parents' upstairs porch," Bruce explained.

"Would you like some, Dad?" Garrett asked, reaching for an empty cone. "It has sugar and food coloring in it."

"So I see," Mr. MacBain said. "Boys, even though no one may have stepped in the snow on Bruce's porch, it's sure to have picked up some impurities."

"Heavens," Mrs. MacBain said, but she stuck a finger into one of the bowls and sampled the red ice.

There was no way Garrett and Bruce could explain that the snow they had used was magical and pure without giving away Mr. Chill's secret, so they remained silent.

"I doubt that anyone will get sick," Mr. MacBain said, "but we'd better close up shop right away." And he and Garrett's mother began gathering up the bowls and remaining cones.

"I bet we've made enough to buy the scarf," Garrett whispered, as he and Bruce lugged the lemonade stand up to the house.

"My dad's going into town in about half an hour to buy tires," Bruce added. "We can bum a ride to The Sports Shop and then walk back home. They have lots of scarves there."

Forty minutes later, after wolfing down peanut-butter sandwiches prepared by Mrs. MacBain, Garrett and Bruce were standing in the boys department of The Sports Shop. They were happy to find that all the scarves were on sale. After careful deliberation they selected a snappy red plaid marked down to $4.99. The salesman was not too thrilled to see the scarf paid for all in change, but the boys were very pleased with their purchase, especially as there was enough money left over for each of them to buy a candy bar at the stationery store next door.

"Should we show Mr. Chill the scarf right away or wait till tonight?" Garrett asked on their way home from town.

"Let's wait," Bruce said, digging his hands deeper into his pockets. "I need to go inside and get warm."

"Want to have some cocoa at my house?" Garrett said, happy to have a friend he could ask.

FORT MACCHILL

At nine o'clock that night Bruce Biggs was cutting across the MacBains' yard at the same moment that Garrett was cautiously leaving his house. Mr. Chill was waiting for them both under the pine tree.

"Hey, I saw you guys giving out snowballs," he called to them. "But I didn't see anyone handing over a muffler." Then he saw the plastic bag under Garrett's arm. "What's that?" he asked eagerly.

"It's the present we bought you with the money we got from selling snow cones and stuff," Bruce explained as Garrett opened the bag and held out the new scarf.

"For me? My muffler?" Mr. Chill asked, taking it in both hands.

"All yours," Garrett said. With some difficulty, Mr.

Chill put the scarf around his neck. It was a little short for him, but he was crazy about it.

"Do I look like Garrett's dad?" he asked Bruce.

"Not exactly," Bruce said, trying to change a giggle into a polite cough.

"You look like yourself, only nicer," Garrett told Mr. Chill. "What do you want to do tonight?"

"I can't play tonight," the snowman said.

Garrett and Bruce looked at Mr. Chill in surprise. "How come?" Garrett asked.

"See?" Mr. Chill said, pointing toward Bruce's house. Both boys looked across the Biggses' lawn to the one beyond. There in the moonlight stood a snowman, a lot smaller than Mr. Chill.

"I'm going over there to say hello," he told them, "in my new scarf."

"Maybe I should take the scarf inside," Garrett suggested. "It's supposed to snow tonight, and it'll get all wet and soggy."

"No way, José," Mr. Chill said, raising his stick fingers protectively to his neck. "I love my muffler, and I'm never ever going to take it off."

When Garrett awoke next morning, he knew at once by the cold white light in his room that it must have snowed in the night. He raised himself sleepily on his elbows to see if Mr. Chill's scarf was visible. The fine curtain of snow drifting past his window had already thickly covered the ground like a goosedown comforter. To Garrett's surprise, Mr. Chill was not in his place under the pine tree.

Can he still be visiting with the other snowman?

Garrett asked himself uneasily. Somehow it didn't seem likely. Hastily Garrett pulled on some clothes, anything he could find, and hurried from his room. In the hall, he threw on his parka and boots and let himself out the front door. The snowman on the lawn next to Bruce's was wearing a mantle of new snow, but he was standing alone. Mr. Chill was nowhere in sight. The snow was almost up to Garrett's knees as he tramped around the side of the house. "Mr. Chill?" he called uncertainly as he passed the garage. There was no answer. And then Garrett gave a gasp of surprise. In the middle of the backyard stood a giant snow fort. It had battlements and parapets, and its sturdy walls were high enough for a boy to crouch comfortably behind. At either side of the fort's entrance a long twig was stuck into the top of the wall. Around one a red plaid scarf was knotted. As Garrett stared in amazement, a snowball came flying through the air, clipping him on the upper arm.

"Gotcha," said a familiar voice from behind the snow wall. Mr. MacBain stood up, grinning.

"Dad!" Garrett exclaimed. "Did you make this? Wow! It's really neat."

"To have made this fort I would have had to start about five in the morning." Mr. MacBain laughed and came out of the entrance. "No, it was here when I looked out the window a little while ago."

"Dad, Mr. Chill is missing," Garrett said, looking at the plaid muffler hanging limply from its twig flagpost.

"Look, let me show you something," said Mr. Mac-Bain.

Garrett followed his father around to the back of the fort. Mr. MacBain pointed to the wall. Stuck in its frozen surface were two black buttons. Garrett knelt down to examine them more closely. A few inches away he saw a rough place in the wall about six inches long that looked as if someone might have carved out some teeth there. He looked up at his father. "Do you suppose Mr. Chill is somewhere inside?" he asked.

"Someone's playing tricks on us," Mr. MacBain said, shaking his head. "But who, or how, or why, I don't know."

"For the love of Pete, what's that?" Mrs. MacBain said as she appeared at the kitchen door, clutching her bathrobe around her neck. "Garrett, put on your ski cap, please. I see it's sticking out of your pocket."

At that moment Bruce came hurrying across the lawn from his house.

"Man, that thing is really something," he called. "Gee, Garrett, you and your dad must have gotten up at dawn to build it."

"Nope," Mr. MacBain said. "It's a mystery fort. It just appeared in the yard overnight. Can you beat that?"

Silently Garrett led Bruce to the spot where Mr. Chill's eyes were stuck side by side.

"I hope he's planning on coming back, though," Bruce whispered. "It would be awful if he decided to give up his life to become a fort."

"Oh, he wouldn't do that," Garrett said, trying to keep the worry out of his voice.

"Well, I'll leave you two to man the ramparts," Mr. MacBain told the boys. "In my opinion, we should call this mighty structure Fort MacChill." And he headed into the house, muttering to himself: "They're never gonna believe this in the office."

Garrett was already on his knees, writing the name of the fort with his finger.

"My mom has a lot of scraps of felt at home," Bruce said. "We could cut flags out of them."

A few minutes later the two boys were at the Biggs dining room table with squares of felt and two pairs of scissors. Mrs. Biggs helped them draw a flag pattern on a piece of brown paper. Garrett made a blue flag, Bruce a red. From a scrap of yellow Mrs. Biggs cut out two crowns which they glued on their banners. Later she fixed them scrambled eggs and toast, worried about the weather a little, and urged them both to come back inside if they felt chilly. It was just like being at home, Garrett thought.

"We could ask some other guys over for a snowball fight once we get the flags up," Bruce suggested as they plowed back once more to Garrett's yard.

Before Garrett and Bruce had finished stockpiling snowballs, two fifth graders, Kevin Vanderlip and Gordon Turkel, discovered the fort from Kevin's bedroom window and came over to inspect it. Then Peter Staley and Harry Dietz, who had stopped by to see Bruce, joined the others. Even the Kilbane twins, Azzie and Beezie, who lived over on the next block, braved a rain of snowballs to come stand halfway up the MacBains' driveway where they observed the fort through a pair of binoculars slung around Azzie's neck.

By late morning the snow had tapered off, though the sky still looked gray. Mrs. MacBain made the boys come inside for cocoa, after which they all piled out again to wage further battles around Fort MacChill. Whichever side Bruce was on, won; he had a great pitching arm. Garrett promised himself that as soon as spring came around he would get his father to practice throwing a baseball to him.

"Hey guys, I just remembered something," Gordon Turkel said suddenly, ducking a snowball aimed at his head. "There's no school tomorrow—teachers' conference."

"Hey, that's right," Peter Staley said happily. "Can we play in your fort again, Garrett?"

"Sure," Garrett told him, feeling very popular.

"I've got an idea," Bruce said. "Let's all go ice-skating and come over here after."

The boys agreed and arranged to meet at nine o'clock the next morning at the pond in the park.

"I'll come by and pick you up," Bruce told Garrett, brushing snow from his pants. Garrett wished he could think of some reason for not going, but nothing came to mind. He had never done much skating and was not very good at it. The last thing he wanted was to look like a total fool in front of his new friends.

"Today was a lot of fun," Bruce said. He reached into the pocket of his parka and handed Garrett two shiny black buttons—Mr. Chill's eyes. "He'll need them when he comes back," he said.

"Do you think he will?" Garrett asked. "I can't believe he'd just go off forever without saying good-bye."

"Oh, he'll return," Bruce predicted confidently. He looked at Garrett for a moment and then said, "You know, I'm really glad you moved here. I mean I have a lot of friends and all that, but not a really special guy right next door."

"Right, it makes it convenient and everything," Garrett said, trying not to show how truly happy he was. He was still worried about the snowman, but as he trudged into the house carrying Mr. Chill's scarf, he felt that it had been an altogether great day.

By five o'clock the temperature had taken a dive. Mr. MacBain made a fire in the fireplace in the den. Every so often Garrett would leave the cheerful blaze and squint out the window. The fort, with its flags flying, still stood on the back lawn. No snowman stood under the pine tree on the front lawn.

As soon as dinner was finished, Garrett went out to the frontyard carrying Mr. Chill's muffler. In his pocket were the two eyes.

An icy wind was tearing around the house, like a big cat chasing its own tail. As Garrett moved toward the pine tree snow was suddenly whipped into his face; for a moment he was completely blinded. Then he heard a plaintive voice calling his name.

"Mr. Chill, is that you?" he called back. Hope bubbled up inside him as he brushed the snow from his eyelashes.

"I can't see a thing," complained the voice.

"Neither can I." Garrett blinked and, there, only a

few yards away in the middle of the lawn, stood Mr. Chill, looking bigger and better than ever. The only thing was, his arms were stuck in the wrong places— one coming out of his chest and the other one on top of his head like an antler.

"I've got your eyes!" Garrett cried, relieved and happy to see his friend again. "Lean down."

The snowman bent stiffly from the waist while Garrett stuck them in, tied the muffler back on, and rearranged the arms.

"How'd you like my surprise?" Mr. Chill asked eagerly. "Wasn't I a neato fort? What did Bruce say when he saw me?"

"We both thought you were great," Garrett told him. "How did you turn yourself into something like that?"

"You could do it, too, if you were a snowman," Mr. Chill told him kindly.

Garrett suddenly remembered about Mr. Chill's visit to the other snowman. "What was he like, that other snowman?" he asked curiously.

"Okay," Mr. Chill said.

"Just okay?"

"Well, he can't talk yet," Mr. Chill explained. "He just grunts. But I'm teaching him some words."

"You are?" Garrett looked at the snowman in surprise.

"So far I've taught him *snow, cold, moon, stars, sky, shovel,* and a couple of other ones."

"Did he like your scarf?" Garrett wanted to know.

"I couldn't tell," Mr. Chill said. "I told him *scarf*

but he kept getting it confused with shovel." He turned his gaze toward the Biggses' house. "Bruce is a very good thrower, isn't he?" he asked.

"He sure is," Garrett agreed.

"And probably a good ice skater, too."

"Probably," Garrett said glumly.

"Are you a good skater?"

"I'm not so hot," Garrett admitted.

"I'd be a very good skater," Mr. Chill said.

"How do you know?" Garrett asked. "You've never even tried. It's a lot harder than it looks."

"There are some things you just know," Mr. Chill replied calmly, looking toward the park across the street.

"I'm cold. I'm going back inside," Garrett complained.

"Okay, I'll see you tomorrow," Mr. Chill said, his eyes still on the park. For once, he didn't seem the least bit concerned about not having anyone to play with that night.

"Mr. Chill's back!" Garrett called to his parents as he took his jacket off in the hall.

"What?" his father gasped.

"Garrett, are you putting us on?" His mother hurried to the window to see for herself. Standing on the lawn was the familiar bulky shape. "Now this is weird," she said. "This is really weird."

"No, it isn't, Mom, it's great," Garrett told her cheerfully and went into the kitchen to phone Bruce with the good news.

MR. CHILL ON THE ICE

Mr. Chill was not on the front lawn the next morning. I wonder if he's gone visiting again, Garrett thought. Can't he ever stay put?

Garrett pulled on some clothes and ran down the hall, almost bumping into a man in a painter's cap setting up a ladder. And then he remembered that the kitchen and the dining room were being painted. Mr. MacBain had rented a sanding machine and was taking the day off to sand the living-room floor.

Garrett found his mother in the kitchen, busily loading groceries onto the table so the painter could do the pantry shelves. His father was in the living room, rolling up the carpet. Garrett doubted that either of them had noticed that Mr. Chill was missing again. He grabbed a banana from the fruit basket on the windowsill and ate it while he put on his parka and boots. If Mr. Chill was on his neighbor's lawn there would be no way to get him back in broad daylight.

Garrett stepped onto the front walk, planning to be stern with Mr. Chill for not returning home under cover of darkness. But when he looked across the lawns, up and down the street, all he saw was the other snowman standing alone.

"Why does he always have to be doing something nutty?" Garrett said out loud. He repeated this complaint when Bruce came by twenty minutes later with his ice skates.

"Mr. Chill isn't an ordinary snowman, so I guess we can't expect him to act like one," Bruce said reasonably. "Don't worry, Garrett, he'll be back again."

Garrett did stop worrying, not because he cared any less about Mr. Chill, but because the thought of spending an hour on skates took all his attention. The other boys were already at the pond, gliding swiftly across the frozen surface. Peter Staley was skating backward, and Harry Dietz was practicing jumps. Harry fell as Garrett and Bruce sat down to put on their skates, but Garrett was impressed that he was good enough even to try such a feat.

"Hey guys, there's this really big snowman down there," Gordon Turkel shouted, skating over to Bruce and Garrett.

"Where?" they both asked together.

"Down there"—Gordon pointed—"behind that maple tree."

"Do you suppose it's him?" Bruce whispered.

"I bet it is," Garrett said, rising unsteadily to his feet. Walking crablike, he set off along the edge of the pond.

"Why don't you just skate down?" Bruce called over his shoulder as he glided off. Pretending not to hear, Garrett plowed on doggedly.

Bruce, who had gotten to the tree much sooner than Garrett, was grinning happily as his friend struggled into sight of Mr. Chill.

"He says he's waiting to go skating with you," Bruce reported, laying an affectionate, mittened hand on Mr. Chill's stomach.

"How long have you been here?" Garrett asked the snowman, so happy to see him he forgot to scold him for wandering away.

"I came in the night," Mr. Chill explained. "No one saw me. Take me out on the ice, Garrett."

"Okay," Garrett said, brightening as he realized what a good thing his friend would be to hold on to.

Garrett got behind Mr. Chill and propped his hands against the snowman's back. Together they glided slowly toward the center of the pond, causing quite a stir among the other skaters as they went.

"This is fun!" Mr. Chill exclaimed. "I knew I'd be good. Let's stay a long time, okay, Garrett?"

"*Ssh*," Garrett warned as a girl in a pink ski jacket skated toward them.

"Can I try pushing your snowman?" she said.

"No," Garrett said firmly. "He'd be too heavy for you."

"See me skate!" Mr. Chill called to her proudly.

"Huh?" The girl stood staring in amazement as Garrett and the snowman moved past her.

"You've got to be careful, Mr. Chill," Garrett warned. "You can't talk out loud like that."

"I forgot," Mr. Chill apologized, then seeing Bruce coming toward them, immediately forgot again and called out, "Look at me!" Bruce put a warning finger to his lips as Peter, Gordon, and Harry approached from across the pond.

"I wonder who built this guy," Peter marveled, twirling to a stop beside Mr. Chill.

"He's some snowman," Harry remarked, trying another jump and falling down again.

"Hey, Garrett, let me give him a push or two." Suddenly Gordon wedged himself in between Garrett and Mr. Chill and was propelling the snowman away. Garrett felt very wobbly without his prop. He began to skate slowly after the others, trying to glide the way they were instead of taking short choppy steps. He wished he could put his hands in his pockets so they would think he was going slow on purpose, but he needed to use his arms for balance. All at once, Kevin came up in back of him, slapping a friendly hand on his shoulder. Garrett promptly lurched sideways and sat down hard on the ice.

"These darn skates," he said quickly. "There's

something wrong with the blade on the left one."

"Let's see," Kevin said, hauling Garrett to his feet. But before Garrett was forced to display a perfectly normal skate, Mr. Chill and the others came flying back toward him with several spectators trailing behind.

"This snowman looks as heavy as a ton of bricks," Gordon said, his cheeks almost the color of his red cap, "but the ice is so slick, he's really easy to push."

"I wonder who could have made him?" Peter mused.

I did, Garrett longed to say, totally by myself. Instead, he put his arms around Mr. Chill's familiar bulky middle and propelled him fast toward the foot bridge at the far end of the pond. The sky overhead was bright blue. Except for the swish of ice skates it was very still out on the ice. Behind him, the other skaters' voices sounded dreamy and faraway.

"Garrett, want to hear what I just made up?" Mr. Chill inquired.

"Yup," Garrett told him.

"Hurray for snow, / Hurray for ice, / Snow is great, / But ice is nicer."

"That's very good," Garrett said kindly. He wasn't going to tell Mr. Chill that his poem didn't quite rhyme.

"Can you make those turns like Peter does?" Mr. Chill wanted to know.

"Not yet," Garrett told him. "Right now I think I'm doing good just to stay on my feet."

"I can make one of those turns," Mr. Chill announced. Pulling away from Garrett, he slid in a clumsy half-circle and fell down on his side.

"What happened?" he demanded, looking up at Garrett. "Did you push me?"

"Of course not," Garrett said, choking back a giggle. "Turns are just a lot harder than you thought."

"Ice is a lot harder than I thought, too," said Mr. Chill.

"Snowman fall down." A tiny boy on double runners stopped to stare at Mr. Chill.

"He sure did." The boy's father, a few yards behind his son, skated up to help Garrett right Mr. Chill. "I swear I saw this snowman take off by himself just now. It was the oddest thing."

Garrett merely shrugged, thanked the man, and pushed off with Mr. Chill. As they swept across the ice together, Garrett suddenly realized that he was skating better. At last he seemed to be getting the hang of it. And when Harry Dietz asked if he could borrow Mr. Chill for a while, Garrett didn't do badly without him. He fell once but covered up quite nicely so his friends would think the fall was more of a stunt than an accident.

"Hey, I have an idea," Peter announced as Garrett finally picked himself up.

"What?" Bruce asked, executing an easy, graceful figure eight beside them.

"Why don't we cart this snowman back to Garrett's?" Peter suggested. "We can stick him in the front yard, and go around the back and play in the fort."

"Great idea," Bruce said, looking slyly at Garrett.

"He's awful big," Kevin pointed out. "How will we get him there?"

"I know," Harry Dietz said. "We have this dolly in our garage. It's like a cart that you stick under heavy objects when you need to move them."

Garrett glanced at Mr. Chill, certain the snowman would love the idea of being pulled along on wheels.

Peter accompanied Harry across the street to his house. When they returned ten minutes later, the other boys had taken off their skates and positioned Mr. Chill at the edge of the pond. It took a little tilting forward and tipping backward to ease him onto the dolly but once he was firmly anchored, with a boy on either side in case he started to slip, it was simple enough to haul him the short distance to Garrett's.

Mrs. MacBain was standing outside the front door shaking her mop against the steps as Mr. Chill came rolling up the driveway. "Charlie, come quick!" she called to her husband. Mr. MacBain appeared at her side; together they stared in wonder as the dolly bumped off the driveway onto the lawn.

"Under the pine tree would be a good spot," Garrett suggested.

"Do I dare ask where you found the snowman?" Mr. MacBain called to the boys. "No, don't tell me, let me guess. Let's see, he was in the park sledding."

"No, Dad, he was at the skating pond."

"Of course, why didn't we think of that?" Mr. Mac-Bain turned to his wife with a shrug. "Doesn't everyone have a snowman that wanders around town?"

"I don't know," Mrs. MacBain said slowly. "I think there must be people in this town who spend the winter thinking up tricks to play on one another, or at least on us."

"Guys, you're not gonna believe this—the fort's disappeared!" Kevin had run around the the backyard while the others were still standing under the pine with Mr. Chill. "There's no sign of it," he said breathlessly. "It's totally vanished!" Peter, Harry, and Gordon raced around the side of the house after Kevin to check out the disappearance for themselves. Bruce and Garrett stood for a moment looking at Mr. Chill.

"I can't be two places at once," he told them cheerfully, "and I can't be two different shapes at once either. Not even a super, stupendous snowman like me can do that."

MR. CHILL PLAYS COPS AND ROBBERS

When Garrett got home from school on Tuesday afternoon, his mother was waiting for him at the front door. She had a big smile on her face. "Are you ready for this?" she asked, and he could see she was holding something in her hand. Triumphantly she thrust a photograph at him. It was one he had taken last week of Mr. Chill, and it was spectacular. The snowman stood out against an ice-blue sky. He looked, if anything, even better than he did in person.

"I can't believe I took such a good picture," said Garrett, staring down at it in delight.

"There are others of Mr. Chill on the roll," Mrs. MacBain said, handing him the rest, "but this first one is the best."

Garrett sat down on the hall bench and flipped through the photographs. Those that were not of Mr. Chill were shots taken back in Glen Ridge. But he was so pleased with the ones of the snowman, seeing photographs of his old hometown hardly made him feel homesick at all.

"I'm going to take the ones of Mr. Chill over to show Mrs. Moon," he decided suddenly. "She was really interested in him the day Bruce and I sold the snow cones."

Garrett wanted to stop on the way to his neighbor's to show the photographs to Mr. Chill but decided it was too risky in daylight. He merely gave a little wave as he passed him on the lawn.

"Wow!" Mrs. Moon exclaimed when Garrett showed the pictures to her. "He practically jumps out of the photograph at you." She squinted hard at Mr. Chill. "I've always felt there are snowmen and there are snowmen, just the way there are dolls and dolls. Only a handful of them are really special."

Garrett longed to tell her just how special Mr. Chill was but knew that he mustn't.

"There is a camera club in town," Mrs. Moon was saying. "I'm the president. Next week we're having an exhibition at the library. I'd like to bring one of your pictures—this one I think," she said, holding up the photo Garrett and his mother had liked best. "I'll have it blown up so we can hang it."

"That would be great," Garrett told her. And he added proudly, "This snowman has a name. It's Mr. Chill."

"What a perfect title for your picture! The whole town is going to know about your snowman, Garrett."

"Mrs. Moon says the whole town will know about you," Garrett reported to Mr. Chill shortly before dinner. Shielding the glow from his flashlight with one hand, he shone it on the pictures of Mr. Chill.

"Who is this?" Mr. Chill asked, looking curiously at the first photo. "Whoever he is, he's wearing a scarf just like mine."

"It's you, Mr. Chill," Garrett told him, laughing.

"Me?"

"You."

"You're sure?" Mr. Chill leaned closer.

"Of course I'm sure. Don't you remember that first day when I snapped your picture?"

Mr. Chill looked thoughtful. "Out of that little black box came this picture of me?"

"You've got it."

"Oh, wow!" Mr. Chill exclaimed. Clumsily, he took one of the photos in his hands and held it up close to his face. "Oh, wow!" he repeated. And then, anxiously, "but I'm much bigger than the snowman in this picture, aren't I, Garrett?"

"Much bigger," Garrett assured him. He let the snowman hold the photograph for a while, then gently pried it from his fingers. "I want to take this over to show Bruce," he said. "See ya later, Mr. Chill."

Day after day the weather remained cold. "NORTHEAST IN THE GRIP OF RECORD COLD" the newspaper headlines read. Though people complained of the freezing temperatures, it was all right with Garrett,

Bruce, and Mr. Chill. Every night they spent time together, always remembering to play quietly so as not to be discovered. When the full moon waned and disappeared, it was harder to see out on the frozen lawns, but they all felt safer in the dark. Sometimes Bruce brought over his toboggan, and Mr. Chill pulled the two boys around the yard. Sometimes they played cops and robbers. "Freeze," Garrett would command. "Freeze is what I do best," Mr. Chill would say happily.

One night Garrett carried out a dish of ice cream for the snowman. Mr. Chill had a lot of trouble holding a spoon so he ended up sticking his fingers into the dish and licking them clean.

"Vanilla is my favorite," he decided after trying several other flavors. "For my birthday, I would like lots and lots of vanilla."

But where will you be a year from now? Garrett wondered with a pang and quickly put the disturbing thought from his mind.

Then something exciting happened to Garrett. His photograph of Mr. Chill that Mrs. Moon hung in the exhibit at the library was awarded a purple ribbon. A photographer from the local newspaper drove over to the MacBains' one afternoon and took a picture of Garrett and Bruce standing next to the snowman.

"You're a celebrity now," Garrett told him proudly. "That means you're famous. Everyone knows about you."

"Is the other snowman a celebrity?" Mr. Chill wanted to know.

"No, he's a nobody," Garrett told him.

"Good," said Mr. Chill.

On the last Saturday in February, Mr. and Mrs. MacBain were invited to a dinner party for Stonefield's newcomers. The MacBains had been asked to bring the dessert, and Mrs. MacBain had spent all Saturday morning making chocolate mousse. Mrs. Biggs had given her the name of a sitter, and it had been arranged that Bruce would sleep over at the MacBains'.

"Be sure all the doors are locked," Mr. MacBain instructed the sitter, Patti Silcox. "There have been a few burglaries in the neighborhood recently."

"You bet," Patti said, looking away for a moment from the television.

After supper, Garrett and Bruce joined Mr. Chill on the lawn. Although they had been told not to stay out any later than eight-thirty, they were having such a good time in Bruce's tree house that the St. Luke's bell tower's chimes striking nine o'clock came as a surprise. Mr. Chill had decided that he would like to try getting up into the tree house again, and this time he was a little more agile. While Bruce told Garrett about the secret club he and some of his friends had had last summer, Mr. Chill practiced climbing up and down the ladder. "Look at me," he kept calling to them proudly, "see how fast I can go up and down."

"I guess we should go in," Garrett said when the last chime had sounded. "Come on, Mr. Chill."

As the two boys climbed down from the tree house, they heard footsteps coming toward them at a fast clip.

"I wouldn't be surprised if those weirdos, Azzie and Beezie, are lurking somewhere," Garrett muttered. "I told you I saw them a couple of times in the backyard, looking for the fort."

"Last summer they used binoculars to spy on us up in the tree house," Bruce said, stepping to the ground. Boldly he shone his flashlight in the direction of the approaching footsteps. To his and Garrett's surprise, a man in a ski jacket and ski mask carrying a canvas tote was caught in its beam. As the man raised an arm to protect his eyes, a sudden "whoops!" sounded from above, and Mr. Chill came hurtling through the air, landing on top of the man with a mighty thud. He went sprawling backward, for a moment too stunned even to move; then his arms and legs began flailing wildly.

"We've got to help Mr. Chill," Garrett cried, and he and Bruce rushed forward and flung themselves on top of the two figures on the ground.

"Hey, guys let me up! Look, I'll split the loot fifty-fifty, c'mon, give me a break!" pleaded a muffled voice beneath Mr. Chill.

"He's just about admitted to his crime," Bruce said grimly, pressing himself harder against Mr. Chill.

"Lucky this bozo really is a burglar," Garrett said breathlessly, "otherwise he might sue us for knocking him down."

At that moment, the red light of a police car appeared on Mayflower Road.

"Here, up here!" Bruce cried, waving one arm. The police car swerved into the MacBains' driveway, stopping in front of the garage with a screech of brakes. Two policemen jumped out of the front seat and came running across the lawn. Now it was Garrett's and Bruce's turn to blink as the blinding beam of a flashlight shone in their eyes.

"That's him all right," said one of the police officers as he and his partner rolled Mr. Chill off the burglar.

"This man has pulled down about six heists in town," the other officer told the boys. "How did you nail him anyway?"

Garrett and Bruce glanced at each other, wondering how to explain what had happened. But before they had a chance to answer, Mr. Biggs was jogging toward them across the lawn.

"What's happening?" he asked looking from the police to the boys to Mr. Chill who, though standing, was listing slightly to one side.

"Seems like these two have caught themselves a thief," said the policeman, unzipping the tote bag on the ground while his partner briskly frisked the burglar, who just kept staring at Mr. Chill and shaking his head.

"I can't believe this," he mumbled. "I was tackled by a snowman."

"I think the guy's got a screw loose," Mr. Biggs observed, as handcuffs were slapped on the burglar.

"What's going on? Did you catch him?" a voice called out. Mrs. Moon in a flannel nightgown and a parka and boots came hurrying toward them.

"Are you the party that called headquarters?" the officer holding the tote bag asked.

"I sure am," she told him. "I was awakened by my little Scottie's barks, and then I thought I heard some-

one moving around in the dining room, and that's when I called you. Oh my goodness, there's my silver teapot!" she exclaimed, noticing the open tote for the first time.

"You have the boys here to thank," the officer told her. "It seems that in the dark, the man ran into the snowman and it fell over on him, giving the boys a chance to pin him down."

"Mr. Chill," Mrs. Moon murmured, looking at him in wonder.

"Mr. Chill?" the burglar muttered as the policemen led him away. "He's got a name? I swear I heard him yell 'whoops' just before he brought me down."

"Poor fellow," Mr. Biggs said, tapping the side of his head with a finger. He put an arm around Mrs. Moon. "Come on into the house, Lydia, for a cup of hot tea. You come in too, boys."

"We'll be right there, Dad," Bruce said as his father led Mrs. Moon off. He and Garrett turned to Mr. Chill with admiration.

"You were terrific," Bruce told him.

"It was just like something on television, where the private eye tackles the bad guy by leaping on him from a roof," Garrett marveled.

"Actually I slipped on the top rung of the ladder," Mr. Chill admitted. "Do you think I'll get my picture in the paper again?"

"Will you ever!" Bruce said.

"I bet we all will," Garrett added, "right on the front page."

DEPARTURES

Mr. Chill got his wish. He and the boys had their picture in the *Stonefield News and Review* the following Thursday. BOYS BUILD SNOWMAN, ZAP BURGLAR, the headline read, and even though the reporter who came to interview Garrett and Bruce got a few things twisted, like referring to Bruce as Ben Biggs, extra copies were collected and sent to grandparents and friends. Garrett thought he'd like to work on a newspaper. Bruce and Mr. Chill decided to become detectives.

"I'm afraid Mr. Chill isn't going to get a chance to do anything if this weather keeps up," Bruce said a week later as he and Garrett were on their way to school.

"Have you noticed the days are beginning to get

longer?'' Mrs. MacBain remarked that night at dinner. Then catching the look of alarm on Garrett's face, she added quickly: "Of course, it's only March. Spring is still a long way off."

But Garrett noticed that Mr. Chill was beginning to thin down. He was as tall as ever, but his waistline was definitely slimmer, and Garrett had to retie the snowman's scarf because his neck had shrunk several sizes. Mr. Chill's spirits, though, remained high, and he was as lively as ever—livelier in fact because he had less bulk to carry around.

One night he said, "I'm going over to visit my friend. He knows lots of words now, even though he still gets them mixed up. The trouble is, he just likes to play. It's very hard to try and teach somebody something, Garrett, when they keep hitting you in the stomach with snowballs."

Garrett glanced across the yard at the other snowman. He was now so spindly he looked like a white bannister on a stair railing.

"Good luck," Garrett said, watching Mr. Chill stump off through the dark.

The next morning as he passed Mr. Chill on his way to school Garrett was surprised to see that the snowman looked different. His cheerful mouth was turned down at the corners, and Garrett's heart gave a lurch of fear. Was his snowman beginning to melt?

"What's wrong, Mr. Chill?" he whispered.

"My friend's sick, I think," Mr. Chill told him mournfully. "He's getting all soft in the head, and his body is getting soft, too. He didn't even want to have a snowball fight."

"All we need is a good cold snap," Garrett reassured him. In the mood Mr. Chill was in, Garrett didn't dare tell him that on Friday he and his parents were going to Florida to visit Grandma and Grandpa Mac-Bain. It was the spring break at school, and Bruce and his family were going skiing. Mr. Chill would be all alone for five days. Feeling a little cowardly, both boys agreed not to tell Mr. Chill about their trips until the night before their departure.

"Wow, what am I supposed to do all by myself?" he said when they finally broke the news. "Bruce, I want to go with you up to the mountains."

"You couldn't ride in a car," Bruce told him. "It'd be too warm for you."

"I could ride on the roof," Mr. Chill suggested.

"You'd fall off," Garrett pointed out.

"And besides, we'll be staying in a motel," Bruce said.

"You don't want me to go," Mr. Chill sulked.

"Bruce and I will be back before you know it," Garrett said, sounding like his parents.

Mr. Chill looked at him glumly, and his mouth drooped more than ever.

"Should we take Mr. Chill's nice muffler inside while we're gone?" Mrs. MacBain asked just before they left for the airport.

"No, we have to leave it on him," Garrett said firmly. "It's bad enough that I'm going away. If we took off his scarf, he'd be really miserable."

Garrett's parents just looked at each other and shook their heads.

Despite the fact that Garrett felt guilty about leaving Mr. Chill, once he had boarded the airplane for Florida his thoughts began to turn to warm weather and his grandparents and the long stretch of sandy beach right in front of their house.

The MacBains had a wonderful vacation in the sun; it was only on the last day that something troubling happened. As they were leaving the beach, Garrett overheard a man telling his wife that the Northeast states were having a spell of unseasonably warm weather for March.

"Do you think Mr. Chill will still be there?" Garrett asked his father as they headed back to his grandparents' house.

"I hope so, Garr," Mr. MacBain said. "But if he isn't, well, you knew you couldn't hold on to him forever, right?"

"Right," Garrett murmured with a lump in his throat.

Next day, Garrett kissed his grandparents good-bye. All the way back on the plane he thought about Mr. Chill. Even if the snowman had shrunk to a half or a quarter of his normal size, even if he were now only six inches high, Garrett wouldn't care. There were lots of things you could do with a mini-snowman.

The car trip from the airport to Stonefield seemed to take forever. Garrett was relieved to find the day very cold; in fact, he thought, looking up at the gray afternoon sky as they drove along the highway, there might even be another storm brewing. He began to worry again as he searched the ground they were whizzing past for signs of leftover snow. There were patches here and there, plus a big dirty mound of it in a shopping center that must have been piled up a long time ago by a snowplow. But all in all, the landscape was not the wintry one he had left behind only last week.

"I think this spring we should get a basketball hoop and put it up over the garage," his mother said brightly from the front seat. And Garrett knew she was trying to distract him from the possible disappointment that awaited him at home.

It seemed the closer he and his parents got to Stonefield the less snow there was. And then they were driving down Mayflower Road and up their driveway, and although there were still splotches of grimy snow on the lawn, under the pine tree there was not a trace of winter. Mr. Chill had completely vanished.

"What happened?" Garrett cried, hopping out of the car. "There should be at least one little bit of him left. It was shadier and colder under this tree than anywhere else."

"Well, I guess he just melted, honey," his mother said, putting her arm around him. Together they gazed silently at the spot where Mr. Chill had stood.

"Even his scarf is gone," Garrett said sadly. He was about to check the back of the house when the Biggses' front door opened, and Bruce came running toward them. He didn't look his usual cheerful self either.

"I'll help Dad with the luggage," Mrs. MacBain said, giving Garrett a squeeze. "You'll feel better after you've talked to Bruce."

But Garrett ended up feeling worse, much worse, when he heard what his friend had to say.

"The first thing I did when we got home today was to look for Mr. Chill," he told Garrett, "and you know who I found on your lawn, carting away snow?"

"Who?" Garrett asked in a puzzled voice.

"The weirdo twins."

"Azzie and Beezie? Why would they do that?"

"Oh, it was some dumb game where they were pretending to be a snow-removal company. They had this express wagon piled up with snow they'd shoveled from people's property."

Garrett balled his fists in anger. "I can't stand those girls, especially Azzie," he stormed. "Did they steal his scarf, too?"

"I don't know," Bruce murmured, staring at the soggy patch of ground beneath the pine tree.

Garrett suddenly remembered the orange T-shirt he had bought for Bruce at The Parrott Jungle. "I got you something in Florida," he said glumly.

"I brought you something, too," Bruce said sadly. "C'mon over, and I'll give it to you."

MRS. MOON'S SURPRISE

That night at supper, Garrett, in the blue T-shirt Bruce had brought him from Mt. Snow in Vermont, sat frowning at his peas and kicking the table leg with one foot.

"Please don't do that, Garr," his mother said.

Mr. MacBain looked across the table at his son. "You know what's one of life's toughest things, Garr?" he asked.

Garrett shook his head.

"Learning to say good-bye," Mr. MacBain said. "But I can tell you for sure, almost every good-bye is followed by a new hello. That's one of the things that makes life exciting—the changes, the new starts. Take my word for it, Pal." He reached over and mussed Garrett's hair. Garrett leaned away from his father's hand; although he knew his dad was right, he was in no mood to take his loss cheerfully.

The next morning, when Garrett woke up, he thought for a second he was still at his grandparents'. Then he remembered he was home, and Mr. Chill was gone. He sat up in bed and looked out the window, half-hoping to see the snowman standing under the pine tree. But of course he wasn't there. With a sigh, Garrett slipped out of bed and fumbled for his slippers. At least it was Saturday, and he didn't have to get ready for school.

In the hall he passed his father, who rumpled his hair again and said Garrett was a sleepy head. Did he know it was almost ten o'clock?

"Mrs. Moon called a little while ago," said his mother as he came into the kitchen. "She wonders if you could drop over today."

"I guess she wants to return my picture of Mr. Chill," Garrett said, taking a banana from the bowl on the windowsill. It would be strange to see him, almost like looking at a photograph of a real friend who had gone out of your life forever. Well, Mr. Chill had been a real friend, and Garrett was suddenly eager to get back the photo of him. As soon as he had dressed, he went down the street to Mrs. Moon's and knocked on her front door. Immediately, excited barking sounded inside the house.

"*Ssh*, it's all right, Hotshot, calm down," he heard Mrs. Moon say as she opened the door.

"Hi, Garrett," she greeted him. "How was Florida?"

"Good," he told her, leaning down to pat Hotshot.

He could see his photo of Mr. Chill lying on the hall bench next to the plaid muffler. It was nice of Mrs. Moon to have rescued it for him.

"I have a sort of surprise for you," Mrs. Moon announced, ushering him into the house.

Garrett picked up the picture and the scarf, holding them lovingly in his hands as he followed her through the dining room, into the kitchen, and out to the garage. Mrs. Moon went to a big white freezer against the back wall and raised the lid. Garrett peered inside. There were wrapped packages of meat, neatly labeled, boxes of frozen vegetables, some frozen pie crusts, and two cartons of ice cream. Lying next to one of them was a plastic bag with what looked like a hunk of snow inside. Mrs. Moon lifted it out and silently presented it to Garrett. Garrett stared at it for a moment then all at once it dawned on him what he was being given. "Mr. Chill?" he asked her in a husky voice.

"Mr. Chill," she assured him. "This morning I saw those Kilbane kids going around collecting snow, and before they could get to your snowman, I raced over and saved this bit of him for you. Garrett, have you ever heard of something called a starter in bread baking?"

Garrett shook his head, unable to take his eyes from the plastic bag in his hand.

"Well, it's a yeast mixture that you add flour and other ingredients to to make bread," she explained. "And from each new dough you save a little bit to start more loaves. You can keep a starter going just about forever. You see, I thought next winter you could build

a new snowman with that piece of Mr. Chill there as the starter, and it would be like having him back all over again."

As she was talking, Garrett remembered something Mr. Chill had told him the first night the two of them had played together. "As long as there is just one little piece of me left, I'll be fine," Mr. Chill had said. And now here was the piece, right here in Garrett's hand. A warm wave of joy and relief swept over him. He looked at Mrs. Moon standing beside him with her spiky gray hair and nice smile and thought what a terrific lady she was.

"This is the greatest!" he exclaimed. "It's the best present you could have given me." And with his photograph and Mr. Chill's muffler in one hand and the plastic bag in the other, he rushed off to show his treasure to Bruce.

As he hurried along to the Biggses' he began to hum, thinking of the possibility of Mr. Chill's return next winter. No, it was more than just a possibility, it was a certainty. It would be like old times, he thought, although perhaps not quite. He and Bruce would both be a year older and so would Mr. Chill. As his dad had said, life was filled with changes and new starts, and maybe that wasn't all bad. Still, it was nice to hold onto just a little bit of the past if you could.

Garrett saw Bruce come out of the Biggses' front door and head toward his own house. He quickened his step.

"Hey Bruce, wait up," he called. "I've got something to show you!"